# Just the Way I Am

*To my daughter Victoria (a.k.a. Elle).*
*I love you just the way you are, full of life and oozing with proactivity.*
*—Sean Covey*

*For my beautiful wife, Jann—I love you just the way you are.*
*—Stacy Curtis*

SIMON & SCHUSTER BOOKS FOR YOUNG READERS
An imprint of Simon & Schuster Children's Publishing Division
1230 Avenue of the Americas, New York, New York 10020
Copyright © 2009 by Franklin Covey Co.
All rights reserved, including the right of reproduction in whole or in part in any form.
SIMON & SCHUSTER BOOKS FOR YOUNG READERS is a trademark of Simon & Schuster, Inc.
For information about special discounts for bulk purchases, please contact Simon & Schuster Special Sales at 1-866-506-1949 or business@simonandschuster.com.
The Simon & Schuster Speakers Bureau can bring authors to your live event. For more information or to book an event, contact the Simon & Schuster Speakers Bureau at 1-866-248-3049 or visit our website at www.simonspeakers.com.
Also available in a Simon & Schuster Books for Young Readers hardcover edition
Book design by Laurent Linn
The text for this book was set in Montara Gothic.
The illustrations for this book were rendered in pencil and watercolor.
Manufactured in China | 0218 SCP
First Simon & Schuster Books for Young Readers paperback edition April 2018
2 4 6 8 10 9 7 5 3 1
The Library of Congress has cataloged the hardcover edition as follows:
Covey, Sean.
Just the way I am / Sean Covey ; illustrated by Stacy Curtis.—1st ed.
p. cm.— (The seven habits of happy kids ; #1)
Summary: When Biff the beaver makes fun of Pokey's quills, his friends help the porcupine feel a lot better about himself.
ISBN 978-1-4169-9423-7 (hc alk. paper) | ISBN 978-1-5344-1577-5 (pbk) | ISBN 978-1-4424-9524-1 (eBook)
[1. Teasing—Fiction. 2. Schools—Fiction. 3. Self-esteem—Fiction.
4. Porcupines—Fiction. 5. Animals—Fiction.] I. Curtis, Stacy, ill. II. Title.
PZ7.C8343Ju 2009 | [E]—dc22 | 2009020744

# Just the Way I Am

## SEAN COVEY
### Illustrated by Stacy Curtis

SIMON & SCHUSTER BOOKS FOR YOUNG READERS
New York   London   Toronto   Sydney   New Delhi

Pokey Porcupine was sad.

Every time he walked by Biff Beaver, Biff made fun of him.

"Hey, Pokey. Your quills look like a pile of toothpicks."

Pokey would go home and look in the mirror.

"Biff is right," thought Pokey. "My quills are ugly.

So ugly, I'm not going to school anymore."

His friends tried to help.

"I like your quills," said Goob Bear. "They're spiky."

"He's being outlandish," said Sophie Squirrel.

"Out-what?" said Sammy Squirrel.

"It means silly," said Sophie. "There's nothing wrong with your quills."

"I fink he's wude," said Tagalong Allie the mouse.

"You're a porcupine—you're supposed to have quills," said Jumper Rabbit.

"Just like I'm a rabbit—I'm supposed to be bouncy."

Pokey went for a walk in the meadow. He thought about what his friends had said.

He stopped and looked at his reflection in Cherry Creek.

He wiggled his quills up. He wiggled his quills down.

They made a nice tinkly sound in the wind.

They sparkled in the sun.

Pokey decided that his quills weren't so bad. "I like myself," he thought, "just the way I am."

The next day, Pokey went back to school.

"How come your quills poke out so far?" said Biff.

Pokey smiled and walked away. He was not going to let Biff ruin his day.

The next morning, Pokey decided he liked his quills so much, he would show them off at school.

All of his friends gathered around him.

"I wish *I* had quills," said Biff.

# PARENTS' CORNER

**HABIT 1** —Be Proactive: *You're in Charge*

I REMEMBER WHEN MY LITTLE DAUGHTER DIDN'T WANT TO GO TO SCHOOL BECAUSE some girl had made fun of her freckles, or the time my son became self-conscious about his ears after a friend called him Dumbo. Ouch! The fact is, our kids are going to hear negative comments about themselves from time to time. We can't stop it from happening, but we can prepare them for it by teaching them that they do have a choice. They can let rude comments ruin their day or they can ignore them and replace them with positive self-talk. This doesn't mean that negative comments won't hurt. They always do. But we don't have to believe them or let them fester. Learning to be the master of our moods and to carry our own weather is one of the great challenges of life, even for us adults. But that is exactly what it means to be in charge of your own life, or to be proactive, which is the first habit of happy kids. We can't control what others say or do to us. But we can control what we do about it. And that is what counts. As Eleanor Roosevelt put it, "No one can make you feel inferior without your consent."

In this story, point out how all of us will have a bully like Biff or sometimes even a friend say something hurtful. And we can choose to let it bring us down or choose to shake it off, like water off a duck's back. In the end, Pokey made a good choice—he listened to his friends and his heart instead of listening to Biff.

## Up for Discussion

1. Why was Pokey sad?
2. What did Pokey's friends do to try to make him feel better?
3. What helped Pokey like his quills again?
4. What did Pokey do when Biff Beaver made fun of his quills at school the next day?
5. Did Biff like Pokey's quills at the end of the story? What made Biff change his mind?
6. Has anyone ever said something to you that hurt your feelings? What did you do about it? Who is in charge of being happy or sad?

## Baby Steps

1. The next time someone makes fun of you, smile and walk away, just like Pokey did.
2. Name three things you like about yourself.
3. Tell your mom or dad one thing you want to get better at, like drawing pictures or brushing your teeth.
4. If you hurt someone's feelings, like a friend or a brother or sister, make sure you tell them you're sorry.

# When I Grow Up

To my daughter Allie, my little princess, who I never want to grow up
—Sean Covey

For Charles Schulz, who gave me an end in mind
—Stacy Curtis

SIMON & SCHUSTER BOOKS FOR YOUNG READERS
An imprint of Simon & Schuster Children's Publishing Division
1230 Avenue of the Americas, New York, New York 10020
Copyright © 2009 by Franklin Covey Co.
All rights reserved, including the right of reproduction in whole or in part in any form.
SIMON & SCHUSTER BOOKS FOR YOUNG READERS is a trademark of Simon & Schuster, Inc.
For information about special discounts for bulk purchases, please contact Simon & Schuster Special Sales at 1-866-506-1949 or business@simonandschuster.com.
The Simon & Schuster Speakers Bureau can bring authors to your live event. For more information or to book an event,
contact the Simon & Schuster Speakers Bureau at 1-866-248-3049 or visit our website at www.simonspeakers.com.
Also available in a Simon & Schuster Books for Young Readers hardcover edition
Book design by Laurent Linn
The text for this book was set in Montara Gothic.
The illustrations for this book were rendered in pencil and watercolor.
Manufactured in China | 0218 SCP
First Simon & Schuster Books for Young Readers paperback edition April 2018
2 4 6 8 10 9 7 5 3 1
The Library of Congress has cataloged the hardcover edition as follows:
Covey, Sean.
When I grow up / Sean Covey ; illustrated by Stacy Curtis. — 1st ed.
p. cm. — (The seven habits of happy kids ; #2)
Summary: After her grandmother reads her a story about growing up, Allie imagines what she will be like when she is grown.
ISBN 978-1-4169-9424-4 (hc) | ISBN 978-1-5344-1579-9 (pbk) | ISBN 978-1-4424-9522-7 (eBook)
[1. Growth—Fiction. 2. Imagination—Fiction. 3. Mice—Fiction.]
I. Title. II. Title: When I grow up.
PZ7.C8343 Wh 2009 | [E]—dc22
2009020743

# When I Grow Up

## SEAN COVEY
Illustrated by Stacy Curtis

SIMON & SCHUSTER BOOKS FOR YOUNG READERS
New York   London   Toronto   Sydney   New Delhi

It was time for Tagalong Allie to go to bed.

Allie snuggled under her covers

as Granny read her a story about a little girl who grew up.

Granny finished the story and gave Allie a kiss.

"Time to go to sleep," said Granny.

After Granny left, Allie lay wide awake.

"When I get bigger," said Allie, "I wanna gwow up too."

She imagined what it would be like to be all grown up.

She could wear lots of makeup

and jewelry,

walk to the grocery store all by herself,

make yummy food,

write her very own book,

go to work,

hike to Stewart Falls,

and even fly to the moon.

"But first," said Allie, "I need to . . .

go to school,

do my chores,

and go to sleep.

Then I can gwow up."

Allie turned over,

closed her eyes,

and fell sound asleep.

# PARENTS' CORNER

**HABIT 2** —Begin with the End in Mind: *Have a Plan*

I REMEMBER TUCKING MY OWN ALLIE INTO BED ONE NIGHT WHILE SHE TOLD ME ABOUT all the things she wanted to do when she grew up, like have a baby, drive a car, and make yummy food, hopefully not in that order. I was impressed with how well she could picture the future at the mere age of three. "All children are born geniuses; 9,999 out of every 10,000 are swiftly, inadvertently degeniusized by grown ups," or so said Buckminster Fuller. Truly, children are blessed with the gift of imagination, which is one of the four gifts that make us human, along with conscience, self-awareness, and willpower. And we should do all we can to nurture imagination, not smother it. After all, this is what beginning with the end in mind is all about. It's about visualizing the end state you want, whether it be in a job, a relationship, or a feeling, and then working to achieve it. All things are created twice, you see. First in the mind's eye . . . then for real. Just ask Helen Keller, Mahatma Gandhi, Superman, or Cinderella.

In this story, highlight how Allie begins with the end in mind. She imagines how much fun it will be to grow up and shop, cook, hike, and even fly. She creates this future in her mind's eye in vivid detail. But she then realizes that to get what she wants tomorrow, she must do the little things today, like doing her chores, brushing her teeth, and going to bed.

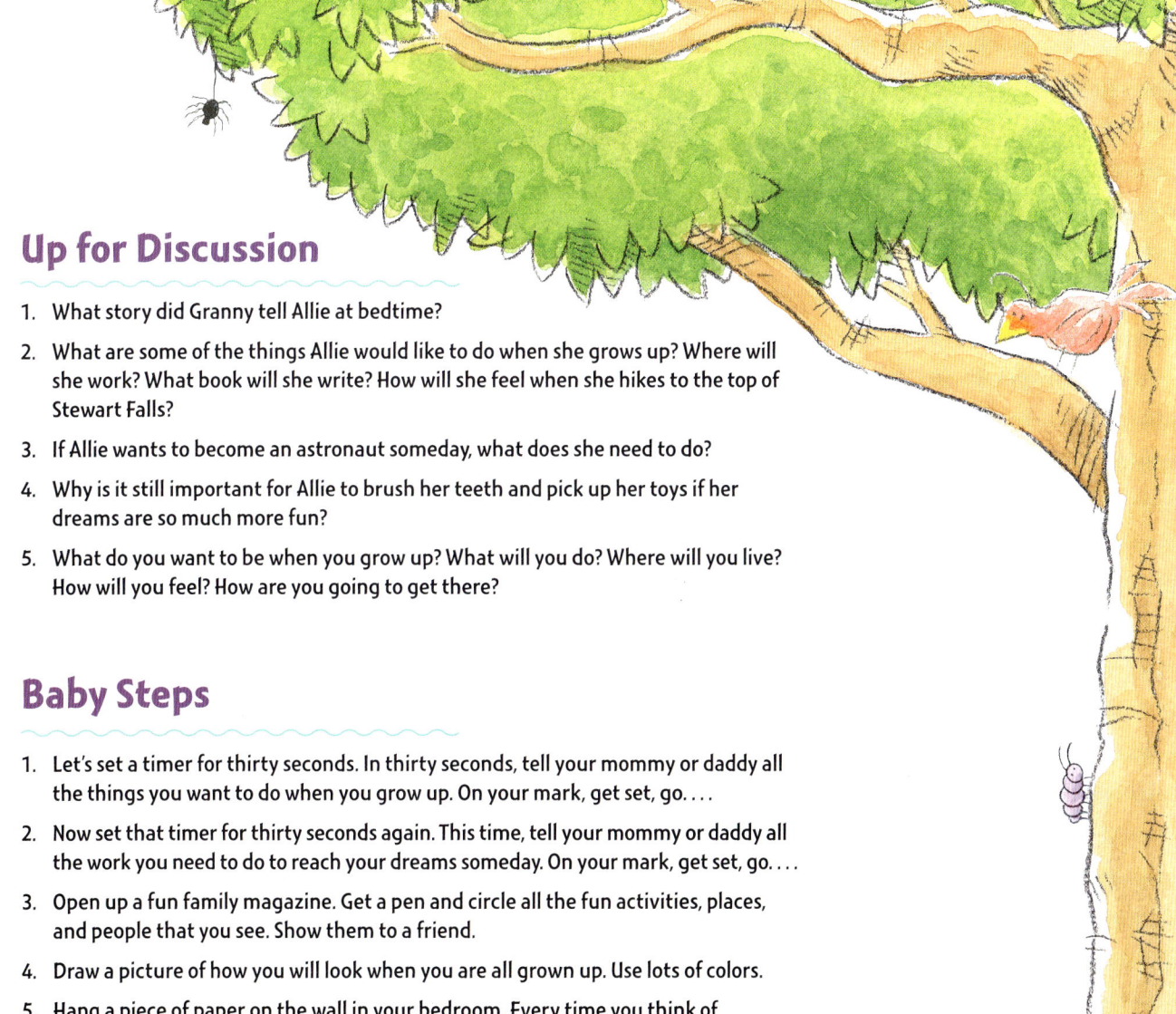

## Up for Discussion

1. What story did Granny tell Allie at bedtime?
2. What are some of the things Allie would like to do when she grows up? Where will she work? What book will she write? How will she feel when she hikes to the top of Stewart Falls?
3. If Allie wants to become an astronaut someday, what does she need to do?
4. Why is it still important for Allie to brush her teeth and pick up her toys if her dreams are so much more fun?
5. What do you want to be when you grow up? What will you do? Where will you live? How will you feel? How are you going to get there?

## Baby Steps

1. Let's set a timer for thirty seconds. In thirty seconds, tell your mommy or daddy all the things you want to do when you grow up. On your mark, get set, go. . . .
2. Now set that timer for thirty seconds again. This time, tell your mommy or daddy all the work you need to do to reach your dreams someday. On your mark, get set, go. . . .
3. Open up a fun family magazine. Get a pen and circle all the fun activities, places, and people that you see. Show them to a friend.
4. Draw a picture of how you will look when you are all grown up. Use lots of colors.
5. Hang a piece of paper on the wall in your bedroom. Every time you think of something new you'd like to do when you grow up, have your big sister or brother or parents write it down for you.

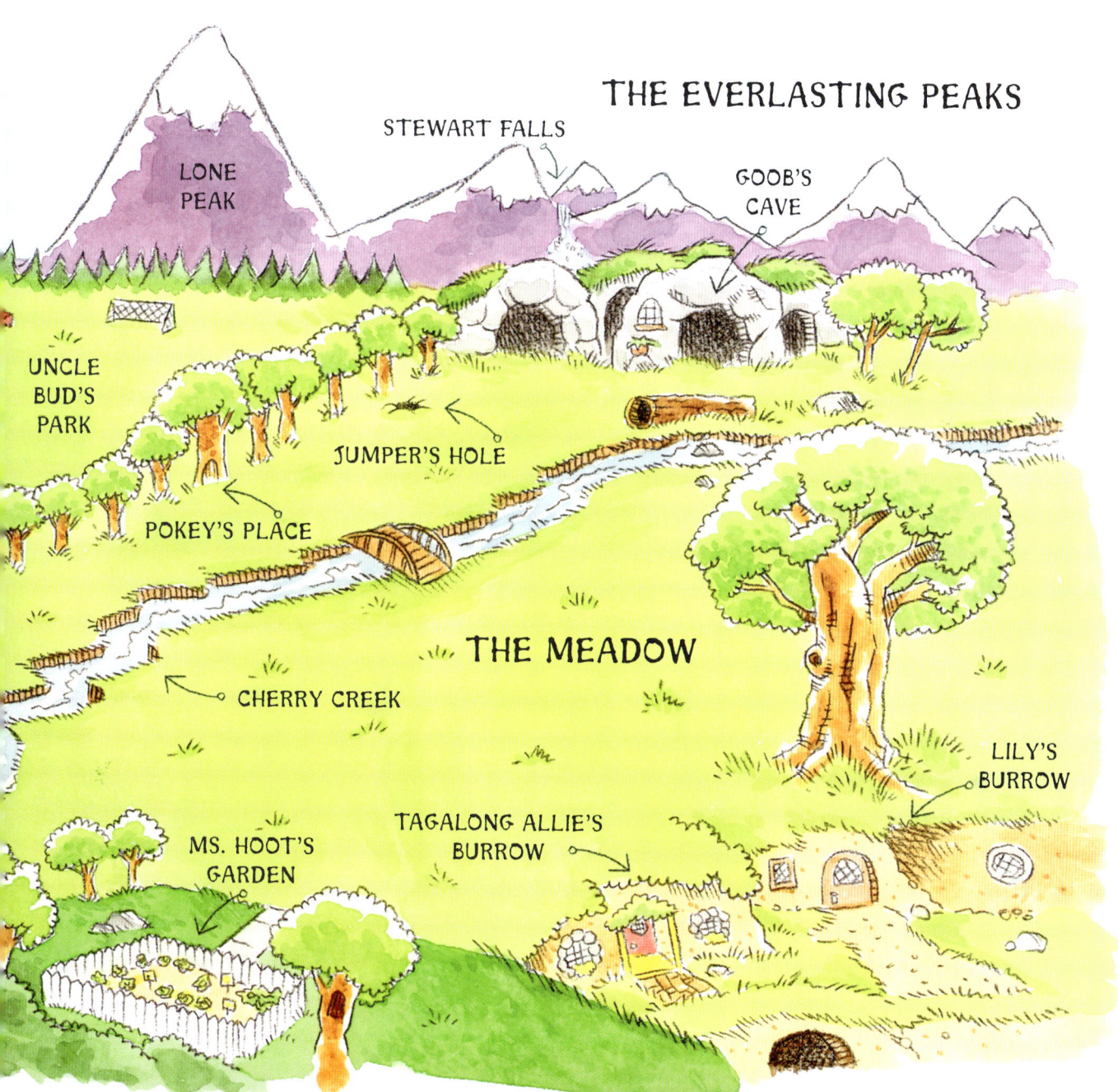

# A Place for Everything

To my sons Michael Sean, Nathan, Weston, and Wyatt: May you never lose your love for good shoes!
—Sean Covey

To my mom, for teaching me to pick up my stuff.
—Stacy Curtis

SIMON & SCHUSTER BOOKS FOR YOUNG READERS
An imprint of Simon & Schuster Children's Publishing Division
1230 Avenue of the Americas, New York, New York 10020
Copyright © 2010 by Franklin Covey Co.
All rights reserved, including the right of reproduction in whole or in part in any form.
SIMON & SCHUSTER BOOKS FOR YOUNG READERS is a trademark of Simon & Schuster, Inc.
For information about special discounts for bulk purchases, please contact Simon & Schuster Special Sales at 1-866-506-1949 or business@simonandschuster.com.
The Simon & Schuster Speakers Bureau can bring authors to your live event. For more information or to book an event, contact the Simon & Schuster Speakers Bureau at 1-866-248-3049 or visit our website at www.simonspeakers.com.
Also available in a Simon & Schuster Books for Young Readers paper-over-board edition
Book design by Laurent Linn
The text for this book was set in Montara Gothic.
The illustrations for this book were rendered in pencil and watercolor.
Manufactured in China
0218 SCP
First Simon & Schuster Books for Young Readers paperback edition April 2018
2 4 6 8 10 9 7 5 3 1
The Library of Congress has cataloged the paper-over-board edition as follows:
Covey, Sean.
A place for everything / Sean Covey ; illustrated by Stacy Curtis.
pages cm. — (The 7 habits of happy kids [3])
Summary: After failing to find his favorite sneakers in time for the big basketball game,
Jumper the rabbit learns how to put his room in order by organizing his possessions.
ISBN 978-1-4169-9425-1
ISBN 978-1-4424-9523-4 (eBook)
[1. Orderliness—Fiction. 2. Lost and found possessions—Fiction. 3. Rabbits—Fiction.
4. Animals—Fiction.] I. Curtis, Stacy, illustrator. II. Title.
PZ7.C8343Pl 2010
[E]—dc22
2009027619
ISBN 978-1-5344-1580-5 (pbk)

# A Place for Everything

## SEAN COVEY
### Illustrated by Stacy Curtis

SIMON & SCHUSTER BOOKS FOR YOUNG READERS
New York    London    Toronto    Sydney    New Delhi

One day Jumper Rabbit bounced by Uncle Bud's Park.

Pokey Porcupine, Stink Skunk, and Tagalong Allie the mouse were playing a pick-up game of basketball with some of the badgers.

"Do you want to play?" they asked.

"You betcha," said Jumper.

"But you can't pway, Jumper," said Allie. "You don't have any squeakers on! Fwip-fwops won't work!"

"No problem," said Jumper. "I'll race home and get my favorite basketball sneakers right now."

But Jumper's hole was such a mess, he couldn't find his sneakers anywhere.

They weren't in his closet

or under his bed

or with all of his sports gear.

Jumper started tossing things out of his hole.

"Ouch!" yelled Goob Bear. "Whatcha doin', Jumper? You got ants in your pants?"

"I can't find my favorite basketball sneakers, and I need them right now!"

"Maybe you left them at Lily's yesterday," said Goob.

So they raced across Cherry Creek to Lily's burrow.

But the sneakers weren't there either.

They looked for them at Sammy and Sophie's tree house,

in Allie's sandbox,

at Pokey's place,

and even in Goob's cave.

Still no sneakers.

"I'll *never* be able to play basketball again for the rest of my LIFE!" wailed Jumper.

"Chill," said Goob. "They've gotta be in your hole. Let's go back and look."

When they got to Jumper's, Goob said, "No wonder you can't find your sneakers. Your hole looks like a tornado hit it. My dad taught me: 'A place for everything, and everything in its place.'"

"What does that mean?" asked Jumper.

"It means you have to organize your things so you can find them. Otherwise you waste a lot of time looking for stuff."

"Oh," said Jumper. "Can you help to magnetize . . . or whatever that word is?"

It took several hours to clean up the hole, but finally they found the basketball sneakers—at the bottom of a big heap of smelly clothes! They also found other things Jumper had been missing for a long time, like his remote-control helicopter and the silver dollar that his grandpa gave him.

By the time they got back to Uncle Bud's Park,

the game was all over.

"Bummer," said Jumper.

"Don't worry, Jumper; you'll be ready next time," said Goob. "Let's not let it ruin our day. Let's go look for ladybugs instead. Have you seen my magnifying glass?"

# PARENTS' CORNER

### HABIT 3 —Put First Things First: *Work First, Then Play*

My son Weston is the king of losing shoes. And they always seem to disappear when we're late for an important date. Sometimes we'll find them by the trampoline, soaking wet from the sprinklers, or in the backseat of the car, stuffed with french fries from the night before. Too often we never see them again. For sure, a little organization would save a whole lot of time, money, and frustration.

Have you ever packed a suitcase and noticed how much more you can fit in when you neatly fold and organize your clothes instead of just throwing them in? It's really quite surprising. The same goes for our lives. The better organized we are, the more we are able to pack in—more time for family and friends, more time for work, more time for play, more time for our "first" things.

This is what Habit 3: Put First Things First is all about. It's about working before we play and keeping our lives organized. Learning basic organization skills is a good thing at any age, but especially while young. That's why we ought to teach our kids that just as there is a time for everything—a time for work, a time for play, and a time for sleep—there should also be a place for everything—a place for our shoes, a place for our homework, and a place for our toys.

In this story, be sure to point out how badly Jumper felt when he missed playing basketball with the gang because his room was so messy he couldn't find his shoes. Contrast that with how good he felt when his room was clean and organized.

## Up for Discussion

1. Why couldn't Jumper play basketball with his friends?
2. What happened when Jumper went back to his home to find his favorite basketball sneakers?
3. What important lesson did Goob teach Jumper about finding stuff?
4. How did Jumper feel when he cleaned his room and found his basketball sneakers? What other missing things did he find?
5. Why is it important to be organized and have "a place for everything and everything in its place"?

## Baby Steps

1. Do you have something important that you always lose, like your favorite toy or your belt or your pocketknife? If so, find a place right now where you will always keep that special thing.
2. Clean your room really well, and then go show your mom or dad. Watch how happy she or he gets!
3. Do you have a place for your homework? If so, then keep up the good work. If not, ask your mom or dad to help you make a place to keep all your homework.
4. Since we have seen how important shoes can be, make sure that you have a good place to put your shoes every night.
5. Talk to your mom or dad about how they take care of their important things.

From the family that brought you
**THE 7 HABITS**

**LOOK FOR ALL The 7 HABITS of Happy Kids BOOKS!**

**HABIT 1**
Be Proactive:
*You're in Charge*

**HABIT 2**
Begin with the End in Mind:
*Have a Plan*

▶ **HABIT ③**
Put First Things First:
*Work First, Then Play*

**HABIT 4**
Think Win-Win:
*Everyone Can Win*

**HABIT 5**
Seek First to Understand,
Then to Be Understood:
*Listen Before You Talk*

**HABIT 6**
Synergize:
*Together Is Better*

**HABIT 7**
Sharpen the Saw:
*Balance Feels Best*

MANUFACTURED IN CHINA
**SIMON & SCHUSTER**
**BOOKS FOR YOUNG READERS**
Simon & Schuster, New York
Ages 2–6 • 0418
EBOOK EDITION ALSO AVAILABLE

Visit us at
simonandschuster.com/kids

ISBN 978-1-5344-1580-5  $6.99 U.S./$8.99 Can.

**FranklinCovey®**
For 7 Habits games
and more info visit
seancovey.com

# The 7 HABITS of Happy Kids

**HABIT 4**

# Sammy and the Pecan Pie

~ SEAN COVEY ~ Illustrated by Stacy Curtis ~

# Sammy and the Pecan Pie

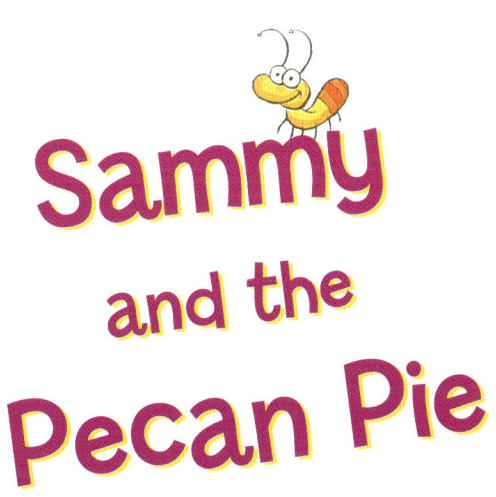

To my intelligent and abundant son Nathan,
who has always been a best friend to his little brother, Weston

—Sean Covey

For my twin brother, Tracy

—Stacy Curtis

SIMON & SCHUSTER BOOKS FOR YOUNG READERS
An imprint of Simon & Schuster Children's Publishing Division
1230 Avenue of the Americas, New York, New York 10020
Copyright © 2013 by Franklin Covey Co.
All rights reserved, including the right of reproduction in whole or in part in any form.
SIMON & SCHUSTER BOOKS FOR YOUNG READERS is a trademark of Simon & Schuster, Inc.
For information about special discounts for bulk purchases, please contact Simon & Schuster Special Sales at 1-866-506-1949 or business@simonandschuster.com.
The Simon & Schuster Speakers Bureau can bring authors to your live event. For more information or to book an event, contact the Simon & Schuster Speakers Bureau at 1-866-248-3049 or visit our website at www.simonspeakers.com.
Also available in a Simon & Schuster Books for Young Readers paper-over-board edition
Book design by Laurent Linn
The text for this book was set in Montara Gothic.
The illustrations for this book were rendered in pencil and watercolor.
Manufactured in China
0218 SCP
First Simon & Schuster Books for Young Readers paperback edition April 2018
2 4 6 8 10 9 7 5 3 1
The Library of Congress has cataloged the hardcover edition as follows:
Covey, Sean.
Sammy and the pecan pie / Sean Covey ; illustrated by Stacy Curtis.
p. cm. —(The seven habits of happy kids; [4])
Summary: Sammy Squirrel and his twin sister, Sophie, usually get along but lately it seems everything is going her way.
ISBN 978-1-4424-7647-9 (hc)
ISBN 978-1-4424-7648-6 (eBook)
[1. Jealousy—Fiction. 2. Brothers and sisters—Fiction. 3. Twins—Fiction.
4. Squirrels—Fiction.] I. curtis, Stacy, ill. II. Title.
PZ7.C8343
2012051106
ISBN 978-1-5344-1581-2 (pbk)

# Sammy and the Pecan Pie

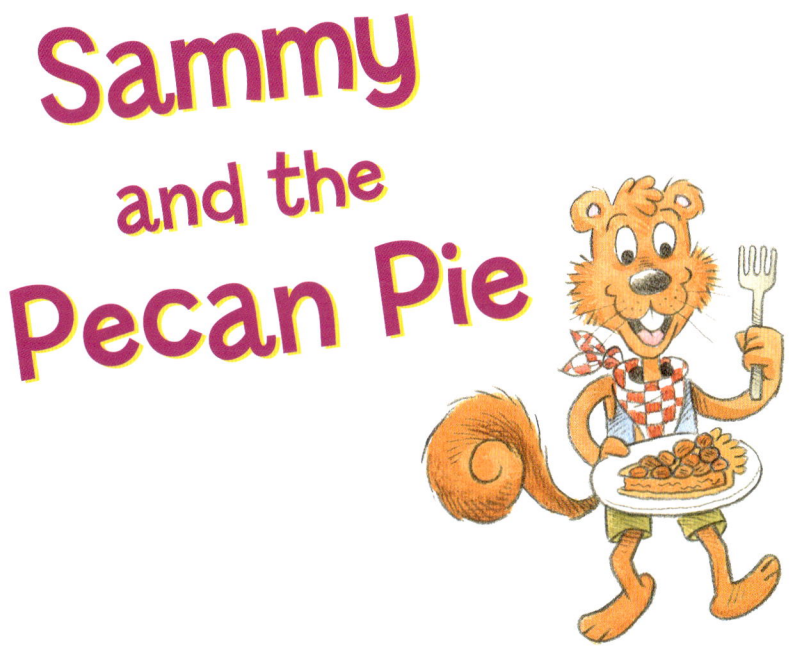

### SEAN COVEY
#### Illustrated by Stacy Curtis

SIMON & SCHUSTER BOOKS FOR YOUNG READERS
New York   London   Toronto   Sydney   New Delhi

Sammy and his twin sister, Sophie, usually got along. But sometimes he wished she didn't do everything right.

One day at school, Ms. Hoot said, "Ruffle my feathers, Sophie. You got one hundred percent again!"

"And you did a good job too, Sammy," said Ms. Hoot.

*I wish I could get one hundred percent like Sophie,* thought Sammy.

After school everyone went to Mandy's Candies.

"We have four dollars and fifty cents. How much candy can we get?" said Lily Skunk.

"A lot," said Goob.

"We can get three bags of yummy gummies, two chocolate worms, and two lucky suckers," said Sophie.

"Wow, Sophie, you added that up fast," said Goob.

"Yeah, your brain must be huge," said Jumper. "Like as big as a basketball."

"Geez, Sammy, what's it wike to have such a smaht sistuh?" asked Tagalong Allie.

"I dunno." Sammy shrugged. "I guess it's all right," he said as he headed home.

Later that night Sammy and Sophie were with their mom and dad.

"Guess what, Mom?" asked Sophie. "The big spelling bee is coming up."

"Oh, Sophie, you're sure to win! And how about you, Sammy? Are you going to enter?"

"I guess," Sammy mumbled.

"I've got a special dessert tonight," said Mom. "Pecan pie!"

"That's my favorite!" said Sammy, brightening.

"I hope you like it!" said Mom.

"Why does Sophie always get the bigger piece? She always wins!" yelled Sammy. Sammy ran to his room and slammed the door.

His mom followed him.

"What's the matter, Sammy?" Mom asked quietly.

"Nothin'," said Sammy.

"C'mon, little squirrel. I know when something's bothering you."

"It's just that Sophie gets all the attention. Everyone thinks she's so smart. And it makes me feel dumb."

"I'm sorry you feel that way, Sammy. But you're smart too!"

"I never get one hundred percent on my spelling tests," said Sammy.

"Maybe not, but Sophie can't build model rockets like you can," said Mom. "Just because Sophie is good at something doesn't take anything away from you."

"What do you mean?" asked Sammy.

"Well, some people think that life is like a pie. If someone gets a big piece, there is less for you. But really, life is more like an all-you-can-eat buffet. Everyone can have all the pie they want. Sophie can have a big piece, and so can you. You can both win."

"So if it's an all-you-can-eat buffet, can I have another piece of pie?"

"Oh, you're such a nut," said Mom.

A few days later it was time for the big science fair.

"Hey, everyone," hollered Sophie. "Come take a look at Sammy's booth! It's phenomenal!"

"Thanks, Sophie," said Sammy. "Yours is good too."

"Wow, Sophie! Your bwuvah is so bwainey!" said Tagalong Allie.

Sammy blushed as Sophie beamed.

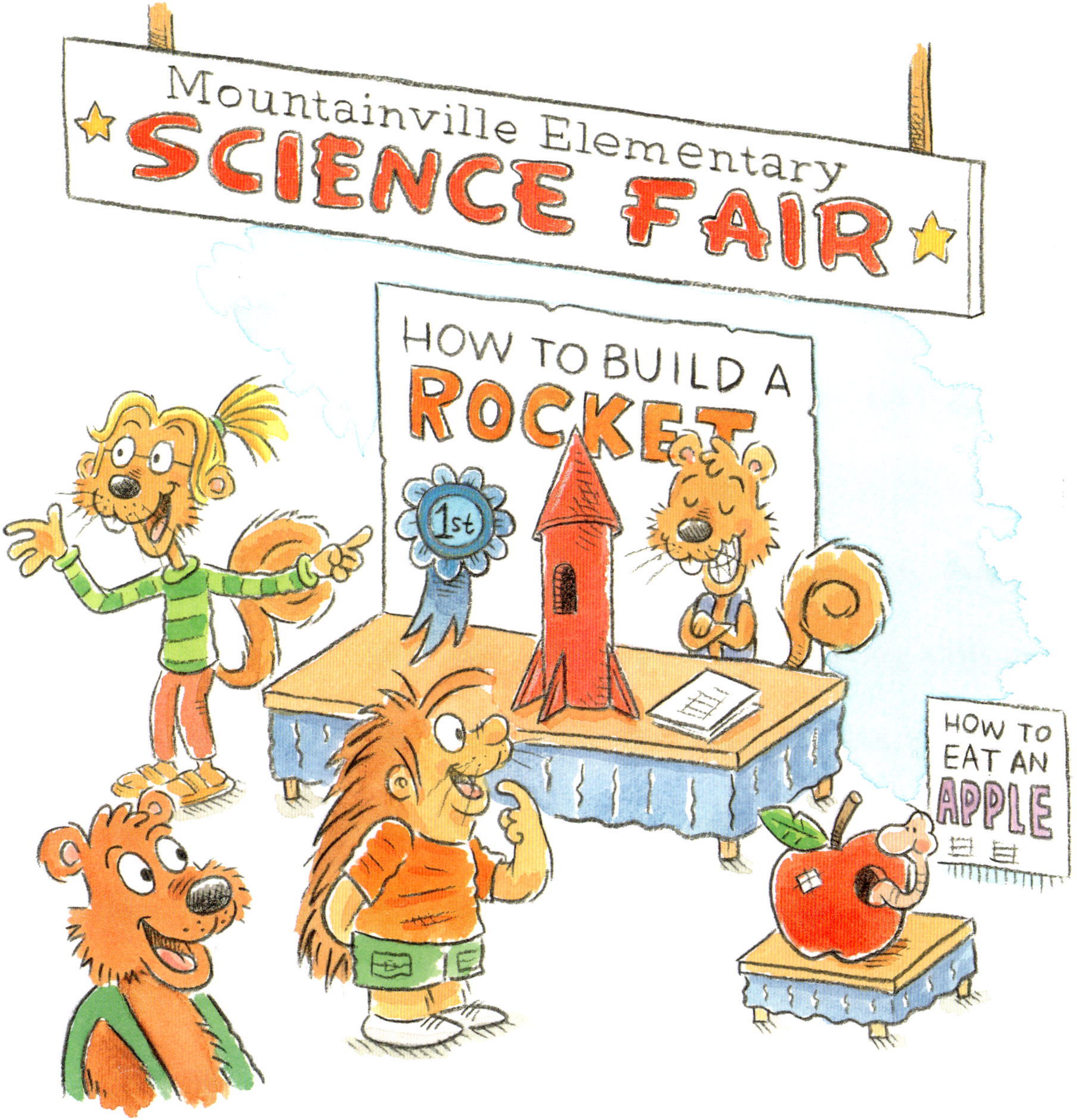
Mountainville Elementary
SCIENCE FAIR
HOW TO BUILD A ROCKET
1st
HOW TO EAT AN APPLE

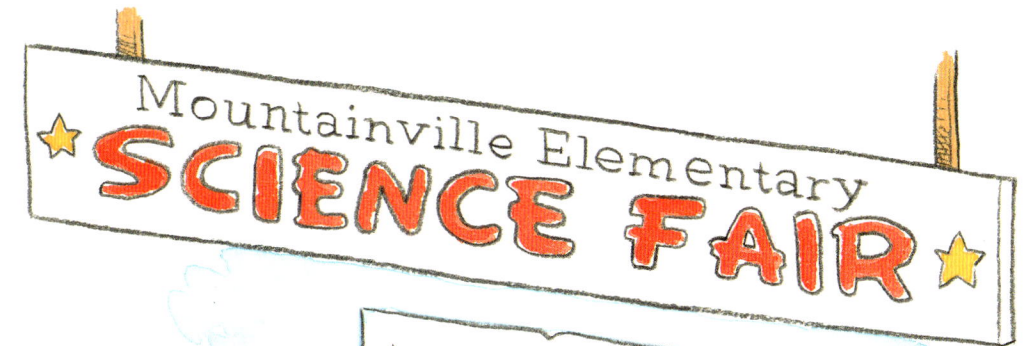

"The science fair was a blast today," said Sammy as they walked home. "I hope Mom has some pie left."

"Yeah, as long as I get the biggest piece," said Sophie, winking at Sammy.

"I think there's more than enough for both of us," said Sammy.

"Last one home's a rotten egg!"

# PARENTS' CORNER

### HABIT 4 —Think Win-Win: *Everyone Can Win*

I adore my two little boys, Nathan and Weston. Three years apart, they are the best of friends. I'm especially proud of the way they attend each other's sporting events to cheer each other on. Becoming jealous of each other's success never even enters their minds. As far as they're concerned, if one of them succeeds, they both succeed. This is the win-win spirit, the belief that there is more than enough success to go around and to spare.

I hope my boys will always feel this way toward each other and their friends. But I know this won't be easy in this competitive world of ours. As we mature, if we aren't careful, envy and jealousy can creep into our hearts. And it is not uncommon to find ourselves becoming threatened by the successes of others, especially those closest to us, as if their success somehow takes something away from us.

As parents and teachers, there is so much we can do to instill confidence and win-win thinking in our kids. First, we can show unconditional love at all times instead of doling out love based on performance. Next, we can avoid comparative language at all costs, such as, "Why can't you do your homework like your brother?" In its place we can use language that affirms a child's worth and potential, such as, "You're so good at that!"

In this story, point out that, like Sammy, we too need to learn to not be jealous or to compare ourselves to others. The truth is, we are all VIPs. There is something different and special inside of each of us.

## Up for Discussion

1. After Sophie got 100% on her test, how did Sammy feel?
2. Of all the candy in Mandy's Candies, which would you like the best?
3. Why did Sammy leave the table unhappy after dinner? What did his mother say to make him feel better?
4. What did Sammy make for the science fair?
5. How did Sophie feel about Sammy doing so well at the science fair? How should you feel when one of your friends does well at something?

## Baby Steps

1. Draw a picture of something your best friend is really good at. Now draw a picture of something you're really good at.
2. Do you ever compare yourself to another person? Who is it? Talk to your mom and dad about that.
3. Play a game and don't worry about who wins or loses. Play just for the fun of it.
4. Help a family member do a household chore. Work together to make it go faster.
5. In the next five minutes, compliment a family member on something they do well.

# Lily and the Yucky Cookies

To my amazing son Weston, for listening to all my wild stories at night
—Sean Covey

For my sister, Shelley
—Stacy Curtis

SIMON & SCHUSTER BOOKS FOR YOUNG READERS
An imprint of Simon & Schuster Children's Publishing Division
1230 Avenue of the Americas, New York, New York 10020
Copyright © 2013 by Franklin Covey Co.
All rights reserved, including the right of reproduction in whole or in part in any form.
SIMON & SCHUSTER BOOKS FOR YOUNG READERS is a trademark of Simon & Schuster, Inc.
For information about special discounts for bulk purchases, please contact Simon & Schuster Special Sales at 1-866-506-1949 or business@simonandschuster.com.
The Simon & Schuster Speakers Bureau can bring authors to your live event. For more information or to book an event, contact the Simon & Schuster Speakers Bureau at 1-866-248-3049 or visit our website at www.simonspeakers.com.
Also available as a Simon & Schuster Books for Young Readers hardcover edition
Book design by Laurent Linn
The text for this book was set in Montara Gothic.
The illustrations for this book were rendered in pencil and watercolor.
Manufactured in China
0218 SCP
First Simon & Schuster Books for Young Readers paperback edition April 2018
2 4 6 8 10 9 7 5 3 1
The Library of Congress has cataloged the hardcover edition as follows:
Covey, Sean.
Lily and the yucky cookies / Sean Covey ; illustrated by Stacy Curtis. —First edition.
pages cm. —(The 7 habits of happy kids ; [5])
Summary: Lily Skunk bakes cookies for her friends without listening to her father's instructions.
ISBN 978-1-4424-7649-3 (hardcover)
[1. Listening—Fiction. 2. Baking—Fiction. 3. Skunks—Fiction.] I. Curtis, Stacy, illustrator. II. Title.
PZ7.C8343Lil 2013
[E]—dc23   2012051108
ISBN 978-1-5344-1582-9 (pbk)
ISBN 978-1-4424-7650-9 (eBook)

# Lily
## and the
# Yucky
# Cookies

**SEAN COVEY**

Illustrated by **Stacy Curtis**

SIMON & SCHUSTER BOOKS FOR YOUNG READERS

New York    London    Toronto    Sydney    New Delhi

"Is it going to rain all day, Dad?" said Lily Skunk. "My friends were going to Fish-Eye Lake today. Now there's nothing to do."

"We can bake cookies," Lily's dad said. "It's a perfect rainy day treat."

"Yum," said Lily's little brother, Stink.

"I've seen Mom do it a hundred times. I know exactly what to do," Lily said.

"Well," her dad said, "let's check the recipe just to be sure."

"First you have to mix two cups of flour, a half cup of sugar, and a pinch of . . . are you listening, Lily?" asked Dad.

"Daaaad," said Lily. "I don't need a recipe. I know what I'm doing."

"Be careful, Lily. You're moving awfully fast," her dad said.

"It's all right, Dad. They'll be perfect." Lily finished mixing and her dad helped her put the cookies in the oven.

"Look, Lily, the sun is coming out!" Stink exclaimed. "You can go to Fish-Eye Lake now. Can I come?"

"No, you're too little. You stay home," Lily said.

Stink nibbled a cookie and said, "But, Lily, these cookies are . . ."

Lily didn't listen as she rushed off to Fish-Eye Lake.

"Hi, everyone! I brought cookies! I baked them myself. I hope you like them."

"Oh, Lily, those look delectable!" said Sophie.

"Puh," said Jumper. "They taste like salt."

"I think I'm gonna throw up," said Pokey.

"Wiwee, da cookies are kind of gwoss," said Tagalong Allie.

Lily felt awful. She didn't know what went wrong. So she went home.

"Dad, nobody liked my cookies and Allie said they were gross and Pokey almost threw up and so I dumped them all in the garbage," said Lily.

"It's okay, Lily," said her dad. "You just need to listen next time. You don't have to follow the recipe exactly, but you want to make sure you

understand every step before you get started."

"Can we bake cookies again? I promise, promise, promise that I'll listen this time."

After dinner Lily and her dad went back to the kitchen to make more cookies. Lily listened as her dad read the whole recipe. Stink tried to help too, but he kept eating all the chocolate chips.

The next day Lily brought a new batch of cookies to her friends.

"These are much better," said Lily.

But no one wanted to try them.

"I'm not going to go first," said Jumper.

Finally Allie said, "I'll twy one."

Everyone watched as Allie slowly put one in her mouth.

"Yup, yup, yup. These are the best cookies eveh, Wiwee!"

They all started grabbing and eating the cookies. Pretty soon they were all gone.

"Those cookies are so yummy for my tummy," said Goob.

"What's in them?" asked Pokey.

"Well . . ." Lily said, "the secret ingredient is listening."

# PARENTS' CORNER

**HABIT 5** —Seek First to Understand, Then to Be Understood:
*Listen Before You Talk*

As Lily had to learn the hard way, seeking first to understand, or listening, is the secret ingredient of life. In general, there is way too much talking and way too little listening going on. Like Lily, we have a tendency to think we know it all, to rush in, to fix things up with good advice. We too often fail to read directions, to diagnose, to truly understand another person's point of view.

Seeking first to understand is a correct principle in all areas of life. A good writer will understand his audience before writing a paper. A good doctor will diagnose before she prescribes. A careful mother will understand her child before evaluating or judging. An effective teacher will assess the needs of his class before teaching.

In this story, Lily thought she knew it all and didn't take the time to listen. As a result, her cookies were yucky. When she took the time to listen and follow a recipe, the cookies were "yummy for my tummy," as Goob put it. And that's how it is in life, too. Listening takes time. Trying to understand where your spouse or colleague or child is coming from takes time. But it also produces a great batch of cookies. And it doesn't take anywhere near as much time as it takes to back up and correct misunderstandings when you're already miles down the road, to redo, to live with unexpressed and unsolved problems, to deal with the results of not giving people what they want most, which is simply to be understood.

Let us always remember that we have two ears and one mouth and we should use them accordingly.

## Up for Discussion

1. What did Lily do wrong while making cookies?
2. Why didn't Lily pay attention to her father?
3. What happened when she gave the 7 Oaks gang the cookies at Fish-Eye Lake?
4. The next time Lily baked cookies, what did she do differently? What did her friends think about the new batch of cookies?
5. Why is it important to listen?

## Baby Steps

1. Ask others about what you can do on a rainy day. Listen carefully and make a list.
2. Have a friend or sibling tell you a story. Listen closely and tell that story to someone else.
3. Talk with your mother and father about how you can be a better listener.
4. Go thirty minutes without saying anything, only listening.
5. Bake cookies with your mother and father and follow the instructions closely. Be sure when you make your cookies that you add your own secret ingredient.

# Sophie
## and the
# Perfect
# Poem

To my daughter Beth, steady, accepting,
and a friend to everyone.
—Sean Covey

For my brother, Jeff
—Stacy Curtis

SIMON & SCHUSTER BOOKS FOR YOUNG READERS
An imprint of Simon & Schuster Children's Publishing Division
1230 Avenue of the Americas, New York, New York 10020
Copyright © 2013 by Franklin Covey Co.
All rights reserved, including the right of reproduction in whole or in part in any form.
SIMON & SCHUSTER BOOKS FOR YOUNG READERS is a trademark of Simon & Schuster, Inc.
For information about special discounts for bulk purchases, please contact Simon & Schuster Special Sales at 1-866-506-1949 or business@simonandschuster.com.
The Simon & Schuster Speakers Bureau can bring authors to your live event. For more information or to book an event, contact the Simon & Schuster Speakers Bureau at 1-866-248-3049 or visit our website at www.simonspeakers.com.
Also available in a Simon & Schuster Books for Young Readers hardcover edition
Book design by Laurent Linn
The text for this book is set in Montara Gothic.
The illustrations for this book are rendered in pencil and watercolor.
Manufactured in China
0218 SCP
First Simon & Schuster Books for Young Readers paperback edition April 2018
2 4 6 8 10 9 7 5 3 1
The Library of Congress has cataloged the hardcover edition as follows:
Covey, Sean.
Sophie and the perfect poem / Sean Covey ; illustrated by Stacy Curtis.
— 1st ed.
p. cm. — (The 7 habits of happy kids ; [6])
Summary: Ms. Hoot assigns Sophie and Biff as partners to write a poem, then encourages Sophie to open her eyes to the possibility that Biff is not as mean and scary as he seems and has some good ideas, too.
ISBN 978-1-4424-7651-6 (hardcover : alk. paper)
[1. Cooperativeness—Fiction. 2. Schools—Fiction. 3. Squirrels—Fiction. 4. Animals—Fiction.] I. Curtis, Stacy, ill. II. Title.
PZ7.C8343Sop 2014
[E]—dc23    2012041833
ISBN 978-1-5344-1583-6 (pbk)
ISBN 978-1-4424-7652-3 (eBook)

# Sophie and the Perfect Poem

## SEAN COVEY
### Illustrated by Stacy Curtis

SIMON & SCHUSTER BOOKS FOR YOUNG READERS
New York   London   Toronto   Sydney   New Delhi

At school one day, Ms. Hoot said, "Class, I am going to pair you up with a partner and have you write a poem to share with the class in one week."

*I hope that I get Lily as my partner*, Sophie thought.

"Lily, you'll be with Pokey. Allie, you'll work with Sammy, and Goob and Jumper will be together.

"And Sophie and Biff," said Ms. Hoot.

Sophie couldn't believe it. She didn't want to be partners with Biff. Biff was mean and scary.

"Geez, Sophie. Sowwy you got Biff," said Tagalong Allie.

"Yeah," said Jumper. "That's a real bummer."

"I'm probably going to have to write it all by myself," said Sophie. "It has to be perfect."

The next day, Ms. Hoot gave everyone time to meet with their partners. Sophie and Biff got together in the corner by the fish tank.

"I think we should write a poem about the sun, moon, and stars," said Sophie.

"That's dumb," said Biff. "I think we should write a poem about trees, wind, and water."

Sophie sighed. This was going to be even harder than she thought.

Sophie decided to talk with Ms. Hoot.

"Can I please get a different partner? Biff isn't very nice and he doesn't have any respectable ideas."

"Oh, my dear Sophie. If you get to know him, you'll find that Biff is really nice and he has lots of good ideas, just like you," said Ms. Hoot. "I'm sure you two can come up with a poem that you both are proud of. Just open your eyes."

Sophie agreed that she would try.

So Biff and Sophie started working on their poem.

"What do you like about trees?" asked Sophie.

"You can use them to make a beaver dam. My dad made one that took him six months and I got to help."

"That's cool," said Sophie.

"I also like the sun, moon, stars, and all that stuff, too," said Biff.

"You do?" said Sophie. "Well, maybe we could put our ideas together."

They got to work.

Over the next few days, Sophie and Biff hardly took a break.

The big day had arrived. It was time for everyone to share their poems. Goob and Jumper got up in front of the class and read their poem first.

"Our poem is called 'Bugs and Basketballs.' Here goes," said Goob.

Basketballs and little bugs
Everywhere you look.
Little bugs and basketballs
See them in a book.
If I had an ant
I would hide him in a plant.
If I had a ball
I would bounce it off a wall.
That would be real fun
Too bad this poem is done.

"Well," said Ms. Hoot. "That was . . . ummm . . . interesting."

Next up were Sophie and Biff. Biff nervously read their poem, as Sophie stood proudly by.

"Our poem is called 'Open Your Eyes.'"

I opened my eyes and what did I see?
The sun, the moon, the stars, the trees.
I opened my ears and what did I hear?
A gentle breeze on water clear.
I opened my heart and what did I find?
An awesome new friend and a wonderful time.

Biff and Sophie gave each other a high five and the whole class cheered.

"Well, ruffle my feathers!" said Ms. Hoot. "That was perfect!"

"Wow, Sophie. Your poem was weally, weally good," said Tagalong Allie. "I guess Biff wasn't so bad, huh?"

"Hey, everyone, let's play some soccer!" Jumper called.

"Great!" Sophie said. "Biff, are you coming?"

# PARENTS' CORNER

**HABIT 6** —Synergize: *Together Is Better*

Synergy is when two or more people work together to create something better than either could alone, just like Sophie and Biff did when they wrote their poem. Unlike compromise, where 1+1 equals 1 ½, with synergy, 1 + 1 can equal 3 or more. It's not your way or my way but a better way, a higher way. Builders know all about this. They know that one two-by-four beam can support 607 pounds, but two two-by-fours nailed together can support not just 1,214 pounds (which is what you'd expect), but a whopping 4,878 pounds! So it is with us. We can do so much more together than we can alone.

The fact is, we are all different in so many ways, and that's a wonderful thing. As Dr. Seuss put it, "Some are fast. And some are slow. Some are high. And some are low. Not one of them is like another. Don't ask us why. Go ask your mother." And if we can learn to value our differences and see them as an advantage, instead of being afraid of them and seeing them as obstacles, we will get so much more accomplished—at home and work, in our marriages and friendships, or wherever life may lead.

In this story, point out how Sophie and the gang judged Biff without really knowing him. They thought he was mean and scary. In reality, he was just different. But once Sophie opened her eyes and really got to know Biff and valued his strengths, and Biff did the same with Sophie, good things happened.

So the next time someone disagrees with you, say, "That's good. I'm glad you see it differently."

## Up for Discussion

1. Why didn't Sophie want to work with Biff?
2. What did Sophie want to include in the poem? What did Biff want?
3. How did they work together to come up with the perfect poem?
4. How did the rest of the 7 Oaks gang treat Biff in the end? Why?
5. What does teamwork mean? Why is it important to include others?

## Baby Steps

1. The next time you're at school, talk to someone in your class you wouldn't normally talk to.
2. Have you ever been left out? Talk with your mom and dad about how that made you feel.
3. Work with another person to write a poem or draw a picture.
4. Plan an outing with your family and include everyone's best ideas.
5. Talk to your mom and dad about not judging people. Discuss why differences are good.

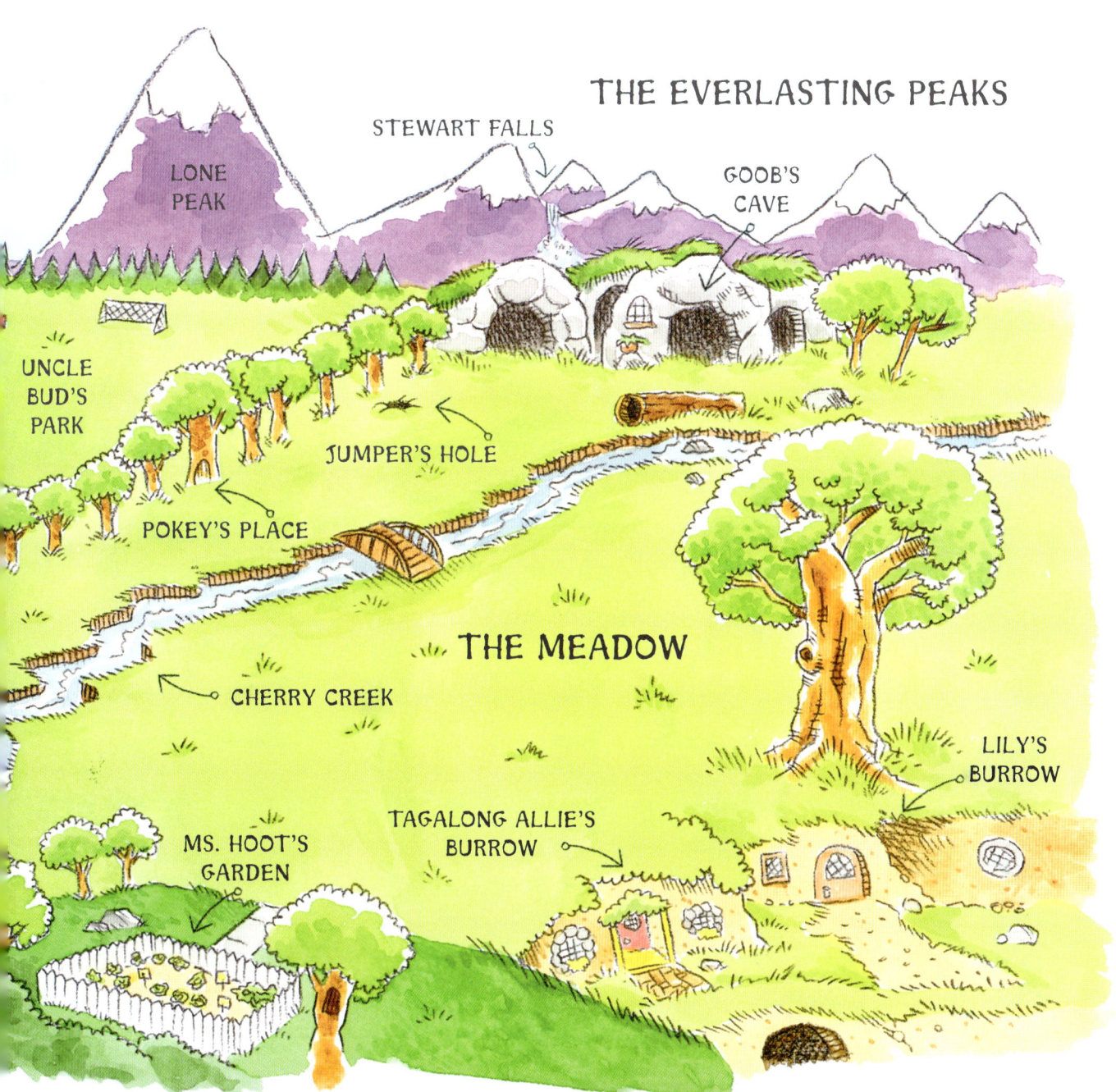

# Goob and His Grandpa

To my precious daughter Rachel, who lived a beautiful life.
I'm so looking forward to our next trail ride.
—Sean Covey

In memory of Mark; you are missed.
—Stacy Curtis

SIMON & SCHUSTER BOOKS FOR YOUNG READERS
An imprint of Simon & Schuster Children's Publishing Division
1230 Avenue of the Americas, New York, New York 10020
Copyright © 2013 by Franklin Covey Co.
All rights reserved, including the right of reproduction in whole or in part in any form.
SIMON & SCHUSTER BOOKS FOR YOUNG READERS is a trademark of Simon & Schuster, Inc.
For information about special discounts for bulk purchases, please contact Simon & Schuster Special Sales at 1-866-506-1949 or business@simonandschuster.com.
The Simon & Schuster Speakers Bureau can bring authors to your live event. For more information or to book an event, contact the Simon & Schuster Speakers Bureau at 1-866-248-3049 or visit our website at www.simonspeakers.com.
Also available in a Simon & Schuster Books for Young Readers paper-over-board edition
Book design by Laurent Linn
The text for this book was set in Montara Gothic.
The illustrations for this book were rendered in pencil and watercolor.
Manufactured in China
0218 SCP
First Simon & Schuster Books for Young Readers paperback edition April 2018
2 4 6 8 10 9 7 5 3 1
The Library of Congress has cataloged the paper-over-board edition as follows:
Covey, Sean.
Goob and his grandpa / Sean Covey ; illustrated by Stacy Curtis. — First edition.
pages cm. — (The 7 habits of happy kids)
Summary: Goob's friends help him after his grandpa passes away.
ISBN 978-1-4424-7653-0 (hardcover : alk. paper) [1. Grandfathers—Fiction.
2. Death—Fiction. 3. Grief—Fiction. 4. Friendship—Fiction. 5. Bears—Fiction.
6. Animals—Fiction.] I. Curtis, Stacy, illustrator. II. Title.
PZ7.C8343Go 2014
[E]—dc23    2012046379
ISBN 978-1-5344-1584-3 (pbk)
ISBN 978-1-4424-7654-7 (eBook)

# Goob and His Grandpa

## SEAN COVEY
### Illustrated by Stacy Curtis

**SIMON & SCHUSTER BOOKS FOR YOUNG READERS**
New York   London   Toronto   Sydney   New Delhi

Goob Bear and his grandpa did everything together. They collected bugs at Fish-Eye Lake. They went on long hikes in the Far North Woods. They climbed trees and ate honey out of beehives. And they loved to wrestle on the living room floor.

"I love you, little Goober-head," Grandpa would say.

"I love you too, Grandpa," Goob would answer. "You're my best friend."

One Monday morning, Goob didn't show up at school. Ms. Hoot said, "Class, I'm really sorry to tell you that Goob's grandpa died yesterday.

Goob won't be coming to school this week. Please try to cheer him up. At times like this you really need your friends."

Later at recess, the gang got together.

"That stinks," said Lily. "I'll bet Goob misses him so much."

"I think we should go see him," said Pokey.

"I don't know if he'll want to see anyone right now," said Sophie. "He's in mourning."

"Well," said Sammy, "what would you want if your grandpa died?"

"I'd want my fwens to be with me," said Tagalong Allie.

After school that day, everyone showed up at Goob's house. He was sitting in his backyard, feeling sad.

"Hi, Goob," said Lily. "We came to see you."

"We're really sad about your grandpa," said Pokey. "He was a really great guy."

"Thanks, Pokey. I'm sad too. I don't know if I'll ever be happy again," Goob said.

"If you're sad, then we're going to be sad with you," said Jumper.

They all huddled around Goob and they were all sad together for a long time. When it was time for the gang to go home, Goob felt a little better.

The next day everyone got together to make a plan. They knew that Goob needed friends, so each day after school, one of them would visit Goob.

On Tuesday, Sammy and Sophie showed up with their walking sticks and took Goob on a long walk in the Far North Woods.

"That was invigorating," said Sophie.

"And fun, too," said Goob. "Grandpa loved to walk in the woods."

On Wednesday, Pokey took Goob to Fish-Eye Lake to look for bugs.

On Thursday, Lily and Tagalong Allie helped Goob get some honey out of a beehive in a tree. Lily was scared of the bees, but Allie thought they were cute.

And on Friday, Jumper agreed to have a wrestling match with Goob on his living room floor. It wasn't much fun for Jumper because Goob kept squishing him. But Goob had a great time, so Jumper was happy. Even Goob's mom didn't mind.

On Saturday, they all came to visit Goob again.

"We brought you something," said Sophie.

"It's a honey-chocolate cake," said Lily. "We made it ourselves. Don't worry. We followed the recipe this time."

"That's my favorite." Goob smiled.

"I made you a cawd, too," said Tagalong Allie.

Allie opened up the card and read it out loud.

"Dear Goob, I'm so sad your gwanpa died. He was your best fwend. Now me and Jumper and Pokey and Wiwee and Sophie and Sammy will be your best fwends, forevuh. I wuv you. Allie."

Jumper started crying and Goob gave him a hug.

"Thanks, Tagalong," said Goob. "That means everything to me. And thanks for being my friends, you guys. I'm going to miss my grandpa. But I don't feel so sad anymore."

# PARENTS' CORNER

### HABIT 7 —Sharpen the Saw: *Balance Feels Best*

I REMEMBER HOW SHAKEN I FELT WHEN MY FATHER PASSED AWAY. I KNEW I WOULD NEVER BE the same. After his death, I thought spending time alone was what I needed, but surprisingly, I found just the opposite to be true. Spending time with family and friends is what helped me most. The whole ordeal reminded me, once again, that in the great scheme of things relationships are all that really matter. Everything else is fleeting. No one on their deathbed ever wished they'd spent more time at the office.

But it's so easy to forget that in this frenetic world of ours. We get so busy driving that we don't take time to get gas. We get so caught up in our work and our carpools and our to-dos that we forget to spend quality, face-to-face time with the living, breathing human beings all around us. That is why Habit 7, Sharpen the Saw, was invented. It reminds us to take time to renew, to unwind, to take a walk, to laugh, to cry, to step back and think deeply, and to invest in our most important relationships.

In this story, be sure to highlight what a difference Goob's friends made at this difficult time in his life. Often the best thing we can do when a friend or family member is hurting is just to say we're sorry and to mourn with them. We don't need to say anything or fix something; we just need to be there for them so they know we care. May we ever be willing to sharpen our saws by regularly spending time with the people we love, in both good times and bad.

## Up for Discussion

1. Why did Goob miss school?
2. Have you ever lost anyone close to you? How did it make you feel?
3. What do you like to do with your grandparents?
4. How did Goob's friends cheer him up?
5. If this happened to you, what would you like your friends to do to cheer you up?
6. When you feel sad, what do you like to do to feel better?

## Baby Steps

1. Write a note to someone you know who has lost a loved one.
2. Talk to your parents about what you can do or will do when your family loses a loved one.
3. Go for a walk and look for beautiful things that make you happy.
4. Draw a picture of you and your grandparents and have your parents send it to them.
5. Learn more about your family's history by talking to your parents and grandparents about your ancestors.